THE GIFTS

OF THE
ANIMALS

A CHRISTMAS TALE

Carole Gerber

ILLUSTRATED BY

Yumi Shimokawara

THIS STORY IS LOOSELY BASED ON A 12TH CENTURY
LATIN SONG, WHICH BECAME KNOWN IN ENGLAND AS
"THE ANIMAL CAROL."

FAMILIUS

Published by Familius LLC.
1254 Commerce Way, Sanger, CA 93657.
www.familius.com

Familius books are available at special discounts for bulk purchases, whether for sales
promotions or for family or corporate use. For more information, contact Familius Sales
at 559-876-2170 or email orders@familius.com. Reproduction of this book in any manner,
in whole or in part, without written permission of the publisher is prohibited.

LIBRARY OF CONGRESS CATALOGING-IN-PUBLICATION DATA
2019936503   ISBN 9781641701594   eISBN 9781641702058

Book and jacket design by David Miles and Derek George

Printed in the U.S.A.

10 9 8 7 6 5 4 3 2 1

First Edition

To JoJo Abzug,
with love from Mimi

The gentle beasts of sky and earth
prepare their stable for Christ's birth.

The ox that stands in the drafty shed
drops straw into a manger bed.

The sheep tear loose bits of their wool
to make the bed feel soft and full.

The birds on the roof of the lowly shed
prepare a pillow for His head
with feathers pulled from downy breasts . . .

. . . mice carry them to where He'll rest.

The cow that lives in the ancient stall pulls a blanket from the wall.

Carefully, the cow and ox
lay it atop the manger box.

Then in this place, humble and warm,
Christ, the Prince of Peace, is born.

Mary counts His tiny toes
and wraps the Child in swaddling clothes.

Then Joseph lays Him down to sleep inside the box beside the sheep.

Outside, the distant stars grow bright.
They blaze like candles in the night.

Shepherds tending flocks nearby
turn anxious faces to the sky.

"Fear not!" they hear an angel call.
"I bring glad tidings to you all.
In Bethlehem, of humble birth,
a Child's been born who'll bless the earth."

The angel's joined by many more.
They fill the sky. Their voices soar:
"Peace on earth. Good will toward men.
Go now, shepherds, worship him."

The shepherds leave their bleating flocks
to find the Christ Child's manger box.

They join those at His birthing place,
and smiles of joy light up each face.

Then shepherds, beasts,
and birds all sing:

"Glory to our newborn King!"

CONDENSED FROM THE BOOK OF LUKE, CHAPTER 2, KING JAMES VERSION

And it came to pass in those days, that there went out a decree from Caesar Augustus, that all the world should be taxed . . . and all went to be taxed, every one into his own city.

And Joseph also went up from Galilee, out of the city of Nazareth, into Judaea, unto the city of David, which is called Bethlehem . . . to be taxed with Mary his espoused wife, being great with child. . . .

And she brought forth her firstborn son, and wrapped him in swaddling clothes, and laid him in a manger; because there was no room for them in the inn.

And there were in the same country shepherds abiding in the field, keeping watch over their flock by night.

And, lo, the angel of the Lord came upon them, and the glory of the Lord shone round about them: and they were sore afraid.

The angel said unto them, "Fear not: for, behold, I bring you good tidings of great joy, which shall be to all people. For unto you is born this day in the city of David a Saviour, which is Christ the Lord.

"And this shall be a sign unto you. Ye shall find the babe wrapped in swaddling clothes, lying in a manger."

And suddenly there was with the angel a multitude of the heavenly host praising God, and saying, "Glory to God in the highest, and on earth peace, good will toward men."

After the angels were gone away from them into heaven, the shepherds said one to another, "Let us now go even unto Bethlehem, and see this thing which is come to pass, which the Lord hath made known unto us."

And they came with haste, and found Mary, and Joseph, and the babe lying in a manger.